HAPPY LAND

Books by MacKinlay Kantor

God and My Country
Arouse and Beware
The Romance of Rosy Ridge
Here Lies Holly Springs
Valedictory
Happy Land
The Noise of Their Wings
Glory for Me
Midnight Lace
One Wild Oat
Signal Thirty-Two
Wicked Water
Gentle Annie
Don't Touch Me
The Goss Boys
Turkey in the Straw
Lobo
Frontier
The Unseen Witness
Spirit Lake
Story Teller
Beauty Beast
Angleworms on Toast
Hamilton County
Children Sing
I love You, Irene
The Valley Forge
Gettysburg
But Look the Morn

HAPPY LAND

Mackinlay Kantor

SPEAKING VOLUMES, LLC
NAPLES, FLORIDA
2017

Happy Land

ISBN 978-1-62815-603-4

To

Sydney A. Sanders

"Hail, Columbia, happy land!
Hail, ye heroes, heav'n-born band — "

HAPPY LAND

The sign above the drugstore windows had been there a long time — gold and black letters, a scabby gilt mortar-and-pestle. . . . It said simply, "Marsh's," and that meant a great deal to everybody in Hartfield.

It meant gleaming old mirrors, and white-topped, wire-legged tables at which three generations of Hartfield people had eaten strawberry sundaes. It meant prescriptions faithfully filled — a place to lounge and joke and smoke and gossip — to read magazines on the rack free — or to play victrola records in the back room at the side, also free.

"I saw him in at Marsh's last night and — "

"All right, dearie; you and Jenny take this dime and go down to Marsh's and get two big ice-cream cones."

"Mrs. Johnson, I think these capsules ought to fix you up. Just drop in at Marsh's and give this prescription to Lew; he'll fill it while you're getting your groceries next door . . ."

11

Miss Emmy, the old maid who worked at Marsh's — Miss Emmy went home to dinner at 11:30 and got back at 12:30; and then Lew Marsh could go home to his own dinner. The only bad thing about it was that there was no registered pharmacist in the store from 12:30 until 1:30; but if any emergency ever came up (that happened seldom) Lew would leave his dinner and hurry back downtown.

Miss Emmy couldn't fill prescriptions, and neither could Chris, the lame youth who was "helping out" since young Rusty Marsh went into the navy. Rusty was barely twenty-one when he enlisted.

Lew thought that not many boys of Rusty's age could achieve the rating of a First-class Pharmacist's Mate as readily as Rusty had done.

Rusty's picture, taken in uniform with his rating showing on his sleeve, looked down from among the calendars and drug charts and doctors' telephone numbers that adorned the wall beside the prescription booth.

Lew Marsh saw the picture, now, as he closed the big drug register in which he had been making some notations.

Miss Emmy was back, so Lew could go and have his own midday dinner. He yelled goodbye to Miss Emmy and Chris; he warned Chris to be sure to fill the chocolate syrup tank at the fountain, if that new bottle of syrup arrived from the wholesalers. . . . Lew hurried down Second Street.

At the corner of Second and Willson Avenue, Lew turned right past the post office and hastened toward meat balls and escalloped potatoes and sliced tomatoes, skillfully prepared in abundance by his wife, Agnes.

Lew was forty-six years old, but he didn't think that he looked it. His hair was getting quite gray and thinner, and he had had to wear glasses all the time for the past ten years, but he didn't think that he looked forty-six and neither did the loyal and admiring Agnes.

Beneath arching elms and maple trees Lew passed briskly along, until he reached the slight hill which marked the end of Willson Avenue, and the pleasant, shabby white house surrounded by peonies and lilac bushes which was his home, and had been the home of his grandparents before.

Lew was raised in that house through most of

his childhood, and Rusty had been raised there
too. . . . Each in his own generation had climbed
that Whitney tree a hundred times and surfeited
himself with fragrant red apples, nourished by
roots anchored deep in the black soil of the Mid-
dle West.

Lew and Agnes chatted about the events of
their respective mornings, while they ate at the
round old-fashioned table in the dining room.
. . . You don't talk about the war very much —
not when you have a son who has been gone with
the Pacific Fleet for nearly two years, and when
you haven't heard from him for six weeks or
more.

They did talk about Rusty a little, though. Old
Biff came scratching at the screen, and they let
him in, and he wandered around the table working his black nose and sniffing and begging in
accustomed style; and Agnes pretended not to
see when Lew slipped Biff the last bite of his
fifth meat ball.

"Let's see," said Agnes. "How old is Biff
now?"

Lew figured it out — Biff was going on twelve. "Pretty old for a dog."

"Remember the first stray that Rusty ever brought home?" asked Agnes.

And as she spoke the words, a girl was pedaling a bicycle along Willson Avenue — coming their way, coming very close — and they hadn't seen or heard her.

"Remember that puppy, all shaggy and full of burs? Rusty insisted that it must be a fine hunting dog. He couldn't have been more than four or five then, I guess."

Then came the ringing of the squeaky doorbell, and Lew's answering journey to the door. Then came the little telegraph girl who had ridden the bicycle, with her pale face and staring eyes . . . then came a yellow envelope and the queer lines of type which were so hard to understand.

THE NAVY DEPARTMENT DEEPLY REGRETS TO INFORM YOU THAT YOUR SON WAS KILLED IN ACTION IN THE PERFORMANCE OF HIS DUTY AND IN THE SERVICE OF HIS COUNTRY. THE DEPARTMENT EXTENDS TO YOU ITS SINCEREST SYMPATHY IN YOUR GREAT LOSS.

For several weeks after that, Lew Marsh didn't stay at the store any more than he could help. He sent down to Des Moines and managed to hire a draft-exempt pharmacist to take charge of prescriptions. . . . Miss Emmy and Chris, with affectionate sympathy and devotion, could run the rest of the store well enough.

Lew and Agnes just stayed around home. Tires on their old Chev were worn thin and smooth, or they might have saved up their gas ration to go on a short motor trip. Things being as they were, they just stayed home.

Sometimes Lew would go down to the store late in the evening, when there weren't many folks around, and try to keep his eye on things — the books, and the drug stock, and the general inventory.

Agnes seemed to snap out of it sooner than he. She tried to plan little things for his pleasure. She suggested two-handed pinochle, and iced tea under the grape arbor out in the back yard, and things like that. They went to church the first Sunday, but that was the only public appearance they made.

Friends and neighbors came in . . . there

was the very bad picture of Rusty, reproduced not exactly to their liking in the Hartfield *Citizen and Express*, and the next week even in the Des Moines *Register*.

Lew sat around . . . he couldn't seem to shake himself out of it. In his mind was one big WHY? Why, why, why?

It wasn't fair, it wasn't right; this wasn't the world he had always believed in. Death could happen so blankly, so relentlessly, so needlessly to Rusty. . . .

It wasn't right.

Chinese could be killed, and Japs, and Germans, and English boys, too — and, of course, a lot of American boys had been killed — but those were always anonymous thousands and hundreds and dozens. You read about them vaguely, and heard about them over the radio. . . .

It wasn't fair for Rusty to be killed. Marshes fought in wars; they didn't get killed in them. Lew's grandfather had fought for years in the Army of the Tennessee. Third Iowa Volunteer Infantry: that was his regiment. And Lew's own father had gone to Chickamauga with the National Guards in 1898. He hadn't been killed, or even shot at, in the Spanish-American War, though possibly the fever that he suffered down there in camp had in some way brought on his weakness and eventual vanishment, when Lew was just a little boy.

Lew Marsh, himself, had gone all through the last business with Company C, 168th Infantry, 42nd Division. He had seen a lot of shooting and had dodged a lot of shells all the way from the Marne to the Meuse-Argonne offensive. But he hadn't been killed.

Now it had happened. A Marsh had been killed, in 1943, fighting for his country.

What was Rusty Marsh's country, anyway? What was Rusty's world? He didn't know life and he didn't know the world — he hadn't had a chance to live. He hadn't ever eaten at the Ritz, or watched the Brooklyn Dodgers play. He hadn't ever seen Hollywood or Radio City or any of those wonderful places you read about — he hadn't ever paid his own rent, or made a scooter for his little boy . . . so far as Lew Marsh knew, Rusty perhaps had never even slept with a girl. There hadn't been a chance for him to taste the complete riches of existence. He was only a young fellow living at home, going to school, working for his Dad, going out on a mild date, having his dreams. And then the war — and then the Pacific Fleet — far-removed, unlisted breadth of water — and arduous work, and maybe seasickness . . . and then, death.

Where was any personal world, any wonderful and worth-while world, for which Rusty Marsh had fought and died?

Some of these things were in Lew's mind (they seemed to be in his mind all the time). He was lying there on the living-room davenport, staring at a couple of cracks in the ceiling wallpaper, when there came a ring of the doorbell.

At first Lew didn't go to the door, but the bell kept on ringing. He thought that Agnes would go, but it turned out that she had gone into the back yard to pick petunias. So at last Lew got up and went to the door, not caring, not wanting to go — weakly and remotely dreading the attention of some neighbor or the brash spiel of some salesman. . . .

He opened the door and looked out on the porch.

"Grampa."

Everything went filmy, and tried to flow away from Lew Marsh. All he could do was stare, and try to whisper the word again.

But Grampa was there, just the same. He looked as Lew remembered him: smiling, screwed-up face with a shaggy gray mustache, grimy little glasses with bent gilt rims, the shabby gray pants, the slight powdery discoloration of drugs on his sagging vest, the old scuffed black shoes never shined, and the Grand Army hat with its crumby cord, which Gramp always insisted on wearing after he grew older.

"Well, Lew," said Grampa, "aren't you going to ask me to come in and set down?"

Lew told him that it wasn't right or sane; people didn't ever come back like that; and no self-respecting Marsh should try to astonish Eternity.

"You died just after Rusty was born, and that's over twenty-two years ago," said Lew accusingly.

"I know, I know," conceded Grampa. "But I couldn't stand it any longer, the way things are with you. You were grieving so hard and so long that I kind of felt that I should do something.

So I told the Authorities that I would like to come and take a walk with you; and they finally consented. Come on, Lew, let's take a little stroll."

Lew Marsh was stubborn. He said that he didn't want to take a little stroll — not even with a well-loved grandfather who had raised him from a pup — a grandfather who had come sauntering up from a generation in the grave.

"It's the least you can do, seeing as how I went to such great lengths to get permission," said Grampa Marsh.

"I tell you," cried Lew spitefully, "that I don't want to take a walk with you or anybody else!" And he slammed the door.

Well, you couldn't keep Grampa out that way — not as he was situated. . . . He made a face, and chuckled, and walked right through the wall, following Lew Marsh into the living room.

Lew sat down on the couch and stared resentfully when Grampa ambled to the window and looked out at the shady lawns of Willson Avenue.

"I see that young Cecil Weeks has put up a new fence along the back side of their property," said Grampa, peering through the curtain.

"Looks a lot better than the place did when the old lady was still running it. Did she ever pay you for all that perfume she bought, Lew — the time she broke the bottles, and then claimed she had never taken them out of the store, or that we hadn't sent them up to her house, or something?"

"Ed paid for them after the old lady died," said Lew, and then Agnes came in with a bowl of fresh petunias.

Lew was open-mouthed, wondering what Agnes would say when she saw Grampa, but she walked right past him.

"Aren't these pretty, Lew?" said Agnes. "We've got so many. Now I'm going to pick a big basketful and take them over to Aunt Sally Ross; she's been bed-ridden all week . . ."

While she was saying these things, Agnes stood so close to Grampa that she almost touched his sleeve; then she turned around and went back out to the garden.

Old Biff came in as she banged the back door; and when Biff entered the living room Lew was certain that the dog, at least, would notice Grampa.

But Biff didn't growl or anything — just walked right past the old man, and sniffed around his favorite chair, and then jumped up on the hollow cushion. Biff thudded his tail a couple of times, looked reassuringly at Lew, and prepared to take a nap.

"You see how it is," said Grampa. "You won't get any help from them. How are they to argue against me? Go get your hat, and come for that walk we're going to take."

They went down the street past the box-elder trees by the Andrews' house; and by this time, Lew was beginning to get used to Gramp a little bit.

He looked to see whether Mrs. Andrews and her daughter-in-law would recognize Grampa when they passed the corner of the property, but they didn't even speak to the old man. Mrs. Andrews told Lew brightly, "Well, it's a nice day for a walk, Mr. Marsh," and that was all.

Lew and Grampa went on down, past the public library and the Congregational and Baptist churches. When they got near the post office, they seemed to be hearing a band.

"I didn't know there was a parade in town to-day," said Lew.

"How could you know what was going on?" countered Grampa. "You just set at home all the time, grieving about Rusty. You just say 'Why was Rusty killed?' and then you ask yourself if it was worth while for you to lose him, and then you answer yourself, and say 'No.' Well, I'll show you a thing or two. . . ."

They turned the corner by Bossert's store at Second and Willson; and there they saw the parade coming down the street.

The funny thing about it was that Lew Marsh was in the parade.

But the Lew Marsh in the parade was only about twenty-two years old, and he was wearing a well-fitting O.D. uniform, and he had a tin hat and he carried a Springfield rifle, and had a full pack on his back, and the Rainbow Division insignia on his left shoulder. He was a corporal, too.

"Well, look at that!" said Gramp. "Corporal Lew Marsh and a lot of the other boys from the local militia company, coming home in 1919 from service overseas. And there I am, with the

rest of the G. A. R.'s, forming a guard of wel-
come or something. I must have just stepped out
of the store — I see I'm still wearing my old
white coat. . . ."

That was the way it was. That was the first
thing Lew and Grampa saw as they walked
around town.

Ever since he went overseas, young Lew had
been dreaming about a girl who lived out on
West Walnut Street. She hadn't written much
the past few months, but mail always had a hard
time catching up with the 168th Infantry.

The first minute Lew could break away from
his grandfather and the welcoming friends, he
hustled out there to West Walnut Street.

Nobody in sight, on the porch. He ran up the
steps and knocked at the screen door; and while
he was waiting he stood and looked at the old,
familiar canvas porch-swing, and remembered
the times he had sat there with Velma.

A guy about his age — a young fellow in a
gyrene uniform with the Indian head of the Second Division on the shoulder of his blouse —

this fellow suddenly showed up inside the screen.

"Yes?" and he stood looking out at Lew.

Lew stared at the marine, wondering who he was. "Where's Velma?"

"She's here. Who wants to know?"

Lew Marsh felt himself getting sore. "Listen, I want to know. Tell her that Lew Marsh is here and —"

The gyrene began to grin. "Velma's tied up, Jack."

"Tied up? Say, what —"

"Tied up," the marine repeated. "That's what I said: bound and tied — to me. The marines have landed and have the situation well in hand."

Lew stammered and blinked. He tried to say things —

"Forget it, Jack." The marine came outside and shook Lew's flabby hand. "Glad you're back safe and — But here's the story. I'm Andy Jacobson — from up in Mason City where Velma used to live when she was in high school. I got sent back with a casual outfit a while ago and — Well, Velma and I were married last month. Hope you don't mind!"

Lew was still groggy when he got back to the drugstore.

He felt pretty low, naturally, and Grampa tried to cheer him up without much success.

Anyway, it was good to get behind a counter in the store again; and good to take off his army blouse. He found one of his old drugstore coats in a rear closet, and put it on, and decided to straighten up things behind the fountain.

He was painstakingly constructing a pyramid of glasses in front of the mirror, when a cozy voice spoke from the other side of the fountain:

"May I have a peanut sundae, please?"

Lew looked at her in the mirror, and then turned slowly and saw her in the flesh. She was small, chubby, round-bosomed, with a sparkle in her eye.

He had always liked girls in blue middy-blouse suits, especially when they wore sailor hats with long, streaming ribbons.

"I don't think we've got any peanuts. For sundaes, I mean. . . . Here's some chopped walnut meats. . . . Do you mean a peanut-dope sundae?"

She laughed. "What on earth is a peanut-dope sundae?"

"Grampa invented it. Let's see, it ought to be in this jar. . . . Yes, here it is. See, all nice and creamy. . . . He makes it out of peanut butter and marshmallow cream and stuff. Say, you must be a stranger in Hartfield — not to know about Marsh's peanut-dope — "

. . . She thought the peanut-dope sundae was wonderful; and Lew kept talking to her eagerly, and he neglected to wait on trade at some of the other counters, and Mrs. Billings squawked at him angrily, and said, "Young man, please wait on me — I want a bottle of Father Tom's Magic Emulsion — "

Maybe the peanut-dope was a kind of magic emulsion, too.

. . . Her name was Agnes Dickens. She was the new Methodist minister's daughter. And while she still lingered at the fountain — while Lew kept her lingering there — Paul Nickerson walked in, still wearing his uniform, and Paul reminded Lew about that picnic they had been planning all along . . . all through those other grim picnics in the mud of France, Paul and Lew

and a couple of other boys had planned just
what they would do as soon as they got home.

They would go out to Briggs' Woods in an
old car; and they'd take a lot of potato salad
and deviled eggs and stuff, and steaks to cook
over an open fire, and sandwiches. And girls. Oh,
yes, they'd take girls.

There weren't many flowers growing in the
woods at that season, but Agnes thought that
they might find some anyway. She and Lew wandered away from the others (who were perfectly
willing to be wandered away from) and kept on
through warm and friendly woods, until they
reached a wire fence.

Cows lay in the shade, in the pasture beyond.
"Oo," Agnes said, "I'm afraid of cows."

"They won't hurt you," Lew told her boldly.
He held down the bottom strand of barbed-wire
with one hand and lifted the next strand with
the other, making a place for Agnes to crawl
through. . . . She wrapped her skirts around
her legs (real pretty legs) and slipped through,
bending her auburn head to avoid the wire.

(Barbed wire. The wire in France was coarser, heavier, sharper. Lew shook his head.)

Well, Agnes put her heel in a gopher hole, and tripped and fell in the long grass; and somehow Lew fell beside her. They lay there, feeling secret and deliciously sinful in their green nest, giggling at each other.

Agnes plucked a piece of sorrel and tried to tickle Lew's nose. He bit the sorrel instead.

"Oh, don't eat it! Silly, it'll poison you — "

"Nope. Good to eat. Like salad or something. Come on — try some."

"No, Lew, I won't — "

"Yes, you *will* — "

"Lew, stop! Now, please. Lew — "

The cows watched them solemnly as they laughed and struggled.

(Lew Marsh, forty-six years old, stood with Grampa and looked at the church across the street. "That's where you and Agnes were married, Lew," said Grampa. "And her own father performed the ceremony. Remember? I got to sneezing when you walked down the aisle. Flowers in the church — autumn flowers. Gave me a kind of hay fever, I guess.'')

Grampa didn't insist on their living with him. He invited them, of course — but not as if they had to do it. He knew that young folks ought to be by themselves. So Lew rented a little house over on Webster Street, and he and Agnes moved in there after a wedding trip to the Wisconsin Dells.

Rusty was born in 1920; and Agnes had a rather bad time of it (they never had any more children afterward) ; so that was the reason Lew was at the hospital all night that night; and also, that was the reason Grampa Marsh left them soon afterward.

It was about two in the morning, and the telephone kept ringing and ringing. Grampa came downstairs in his long nightshirt and answered. The call wasn't from Lew — it was from Mrs. Billings. Her husband had just suffered another bad spell, and the prescription ordered by Doc Hammond earlier that week was all used up.

The prescription needed to be refilled immediately. Mr. Billings was suffering agonies; and

Mrs. Billings wailed tearfully that she couldn't get hold of Doc Hammond on the phone. If Lew wouldn't mind going down to the drugstore right away, she'd send her nephew for the medicine and —

"Lew's not here," said Grampa. "He's up at the hospital, and I reckon that's where Doc Hammond is, too. Now don't fret, Mrs. Billings. I'll hustle right down there to the store my own self, and refill that prescription for Walter. You send your nephew in an hour and it'll be all ready."

It was nearly three-quarters of a mile, down to Marsh's. And raining — a cold, steady, raw rain. Grampa's round shoulders were soaked by the time he reached the store, and his feet were wet. He turned on the light behind the prescription desk, and opened the file. . . . All the time, he kept shivering.

He was seventy-eight years old.

Grampa got to see young Russell before he went. Pneumonia isn't that quick, even with the old.

He whispered, "Mighty red of face, isn't he? And reddish hair — guess you ought to call him Rusty." And, more feebly, "Hello there, Rusty. . . ."

They always took Rusty with them on the morning of each Decoration Day, when they went to the cemetery to fix up the lot — to put big bunches of iris and snowballs and late lilacs on the graves.

Some few of the stores remained open in Hartfield, on Decoration Day, but not Marsh's.

Rusty wanted to know why there were all those flags around.

"That's where the soldiers are sleeping, Rusty. Each one of those graves is where a soldier is buried."

"We got two," said Russell T. Marsh, pointing proudly.

"Yes. That's Grampa. Your great-grandfather. He was a soldier in the Civil War. . . . And this one over here is your grandfather — my own dad. He was in the army at the time of the Spanish-American War."

"Will you have a flag, Pop, when you get died?"

"Sure! You bet I will. I'll have a dandy."

Rusty said, "I want one."

"No telling," said Lew, frowning over his grass-shears, "you might have one by that time."

Agnes cried, "Why, Lew. Don't tell him such things!"

"Well, he might."

Agnes told Rusty, "No, honey. We hope you never have to have a flag. We all hope there'll never, never be another dreadful war— not as long as any of us is alive. Now, here — bring Mamma that big bunch of bleeding-hearts from the basket. . . ."

Lew could remember how she said that . . . all the time they stood listening to the outdoor services — all the time the fife-and-drum corps played, and while the chaplain prayed and the quartet sang and the shaggy line of old soldiers stared and listened, and while all of Hartfield watched reverently . . . no more war. That was right. That was the way an American kid should be brought up — not to dream of gaudy conquests and campaigns.

But to dream of the homely green world in which he lived — a world where the corn grew tall.

In this tall corn, when it was drying in the first coolness of early September, Rusty ran and played Indian. Followed by another little boy and a girl, he whooped his way through the long straight rows that stretched down a hill behind the old Marsh house — the house where Grampa had lived, where Lew and Agnes and Rusty lived now.

It was after supper . . . pale blue mists came up from the Boone River; it was time for children to be in bed. But in those same mists the Sauks had ridden . . . this was dark ground on which Sioux and Pottawatomies had built their fires.

("That's one thing," said Grampa to the modern Lew Marsh, as they stood in ghostly corn and watched the ghostly children. "Kids could always do that in America. They could always play Indian. War clubs, Daniel Boone, Sitting Bull, Buffalo Bill . . . oh yes, I reckon it wouldn't have been proper for kids in other countries to really play Indian. It wouldn't have looked natural. . . . You know, Lew, that's one thing God intended in America, forever. Kids have got to play Indian — always. Nobody must be allowed to make them stop. . . .")

Maybe he didn't have young Agnes Marsh in

mind, but at that very moment she came out of the yard. "Hoo-hoo," she kept calling, as she walked through the corn. "Rusty — Rusty — it's bedtime. Hey, where are you? Answer me."

Rusty got up from concealment in the corn-stalks, followed by his fellow tribesmen. He held up one grubby hand in a gesture of friendship. "Me no Rusty, woman. Me big chief. Ugh!"

Agnes looked pretty, standing there with sunset on her hair. "Ugh," she said, "me squaw. You come with squaw to wigwam — maybe lie on blanket. Great White Father send for you. Other Indians maybe go to their home villages. Ugh!"

In this way she lured him to the house, and up to his high old bed in the little room next to hers and Lew's.

She lay beside him after he was in bed.

". . . And, just think: day-after-tomorrow my big boy will go to school for the first time!"

"Why do I have to go to school, Mamma?"

"It's kindergarten. That's where you start to school, at first."

"Why do they call it that? That's a funny word — "

"Kindergarten? It's a German word."

"What's German?"

"There's a country, far across the sea, where Germans live. And they speak another language, different from ours."

Rusty whispered drowsily, "Oh, yes, Daddy fought Germans in the war. When I get big I'm going to kill a lot of Germans."

"Oh, no," said Agnes decisively, "you are not! Because we are friends of the Germans again. They had a bad old king, dear, called the Kaiser, who wanted to make war against the whole world. But now the Kaiser is gone from Germany, and we are at peace, and probably we always will be."

"What do Germans look like, Mamma?"

"Well, you know nice old Mr. Gerber, over on Cedar Street? Patsy's grandfather? Well, Patsy's grandfather is a German — he used to be a German, he came all the way from Germany long ago, but now he is an American. And little Mrs. Rasch — and Mr. and Mrs. Ziehl — they all came from Germany. . . . You know, Rusty, in Germany there are fine teachers and wonderful, wonderful schools. And great doctors, and men who make beautiful music; oh yes, many of the

Germans are splendid, kind people. . . . And one time, some of the teachers decided that it was hard for little children to have their first learning from big dull books and maps, in dark rooms. So they made a wonderful place for children to start to school in — bright sunshine, and pretty colored papers, and scissors to cut things out, and colored crayons to make pretty pictures — And they called it 'kindergarten,' which means in our language 'child's garden.' Now they have places like that all over the civilized world — and that means almost everywhere, you see. And we have a kindergarten right here in Hartfield, just like the Germans have — a place for children to learn in, and sing in — to learn to make things, and to play new games — and that's the way school begins. You'll love it when you start day-after-tomorrow."

There were Miss Belle and Miss Margie. Miss Belle was old and jolly, and Miss Margie was young — she seemed just like a little girl herself, and Rusty thought she was beautiful when she took his hand and led him around the circle.

The children all sat in red chairs arranged in

a large circle. They sang, "Good morning to you, good morning to you, good morning, dear teachers, good morning to you. . . ."

("Better'n the school I first started to," whispered Grampa Marsh to Lew. "I tell you, Lew, the world is getting better in spite of everything. Why, the first day I started to school — nearly a hundred years ago, now — the master basted my bottom with a hickory stick because I accidentally upset the water bucket. . . .")

There were two little boys sitting next to Rusty: new boys in the public kindergarten, like himself. But whereas Rusty had a crisp new blouse and neat blue pants, these boys were dressed in ragged old overalls, and their hair wasn't even combed; and they smelled funny, too.

Their names were Jacky and Tod, they told him.

"Where do you live?"

"Oh, we live in an old house out by the fairgrounds. We just moved here from Dakota."

They had pinched faces — pale, eager faces . . . you could see that, after Miss Belle took them out in the hall and gently washed off the dirt that had covered them.

"Do you like ice-cream?" asked Rusty.

"I had some once," said Jacky. "Tod — he's littler than me — he never had none."

Rusty gasped, "What? Never had any?"

"Once I had a Hershey bar," Tod told him proudly.

Rusty boasted, "My father — he's got a store just full of ice-cream and stuff. I bet he's got a thousand old Hershey bars and a million thousand tons of ice-cream. All kinds: my father's got chocolate and strawberry and vanilla and maple-pecan and orange and — "

Well, they couldn't believe that, naturally; though their eyes stuck out and their pinched noses quivered at the very idea.

Kindergarten hadn't "let out" more than ten minutes when there was a light scuffling of six small feet in the back room of Marsh's, and Lew looked down in astonishment at three faces — one beaming with satisfaction, the other two white with fear and anticipation.

"Papa," said Rusty, "this is Jacky and Tod.

Jacky only had ice-cream once, and Tod never had any."

. . . It was remarkable how much ice-cream those two ragged kids could eat, sitting there at the fountain, and how catholic were their tastes. Maple, chocolate, cherry: all was grist that came to their mill — until Lew was actually afraid to give them any more.

He let Rusty help them select some candy bars, while he announced over the phone, to Agnes, the result of his judicious questioning.

"Yes, I guess maybe you'd better take the car and run out there. It must be that old shack beyond the Halton place; they say their father's a ditcher, but hasn't been able to work lately, and I guess their mother's got a new baby too. . . . They look at least three-quarters starved. Better take a lot of clean rags and things . . . got any of that stew left from yesterday? A whole kettleful? Good . . . you stop at Sheldon's grocery, and I'll call him and tell him to have a basket of stuff waiting: you know — flour and bacon and eggs and milk and stuff — "

He didn't know that Rusty was there beside him. He didn't know that Jacky and Tod were gone — until he felt a small hand twisting his trouser leg, and looked down to see his son.

"Papa. . . ."

"Yes?"

"Was that for those poor kids?"

"Was what for the poor kids? Are they gone, Rusty?"

"Yes, they went home now. I mean — those things you were talking about with Mamma: stew and bacon and things — "

Lew felt a little shy as the big, solemn eyes looked up at him. "You know, Rus, sometimes people have to do that. Because they want to, I mean. When you see a fellow that hasn't got anything — and you've got things — why, you just give some of your things to him. Some folks call it charity. Me — I don't like the word so well. . . . Maybe it's just being friendly. You ought to be friendly with folks, Rusty. That's what my Gramp always taught me."

Rusty said, "Can I help?"

"Do what?"

"Just help you, Pop — I mean, be friendly with you. Can I, Pop? You have to work real hard, I think, and I want to help you."

Lew laughed, though his eyes felt a little wet suddenly. "O.K. You grab that broom, and begin to sweep. You can help me sweep out the back room."

Rusty took the big broom and began to sweep furiously, eagerly. He was helping Dad.

He helped Dad for a real long time. (As Lew Marsh and Grampa looked on, Rusty grew taller and longer — his clothes changed, and the shape of his head and face changed a little, too.)

He was at least twelve years old, or thereabouts. And Lew, as now observed behind the cigar counter, had lost some hair and put on specs.

Marsh's looked much the same, though there were fewer magazines on the racks and fewer drugs on the shelves. This was the rock bottom of the Depression, now; and the Depression started a lot earlier in the farming states than it did farther east.

It had been a long pull; business was still as slow as molasses in January; but Marsh's drugstore managed to hang on.

The store wasn't the only place where Rusty

worked. The store wasn't fetching in very much money in those days, with collections slow and the farm people unable to come to town and buy much. From the start, Lew had paid Rusty a small wage for things he did around the store on Saturdays, and before and after school during the week; but at this ripe age of twelve Rusty had developed a certain economic consciousness as, perforce, millions of other American little boys had to do. He staunchly refused to take any extra money from his father, as his duties and responsibilities increased.

Rus had a bicycle, so during the after-school hours he would deliver the Hartfield *Citizen and Express* to a route of subscribers. He got two dollars a week for this chore, and, by mutual family consent, one dollar of his wage was turned into the family exchequer. That way Rusty considered that he was helping out at home. Lew felt badly about it, although he recognized the necessity; but sometimes Agnes thought that it was a pretty good thing. She told Lew so. She said that it would give Rusty a sense of family responsibility, and probably she was right.

This particular day was to be a big day in

Rusty's life. On this evening he was to be formally sworn in as a member of the Owl Patrol, Troop One, Boy Scouts of America.

The ceremony took place on the third floor of the primary-school building which had served as the town's Boy Scout headquarters for nearly twenty years. It was an open meeting. They held these twice a year, once in the spring and once in the fall so that the parents of the boys could see.

The Scout hall was a barn-like place which would have been gloomy but for the pennants and home-framed snapshots and colorful charts fastened over the walls. Along one side of the room was a row of glass cases made by the Scouts themselves, and filled with their nature collection. Autumn leaves, pressed wildflowers, chunks of glacial rock, snakes in glass jars — the fauna and mineralogy of mid-America were represented there — together with arrowheads and broken pieces of prehistoric implements which the boys had found.

Lew Marsh and Agnes examined the collection. Vaguely Lew sensed that by accumulating and studying and loving such things, all of the

Scouts might realize that America was a much older and more important place than Hartfield civilization sometimes made it seem.

And there was the service flag from the World War, hanging in dusty pride above an alcove: all those blue stars represented former Scouts who had served in the war. Lew was a little old to be in the Scouts when they organized the first bunch there in town, but some of the younger fellows in Company C had been members of the troop. . . . Lew knew who those three gold stars were, too.

He told Rusty about them as they examined the flag before the meeting officially opened.

"Three of them, Rusty. One would be for Myron Hahne. He died with the flu, down there at Ames. And that next one might be for Benny Billings — he got drowned in the navy — washed off a mine-sweeper or something like that. And the third one: that's Morton Blitzstein."

Rusty stood very straight and solemn, looking at the flag. "Do you mean Blitzstein's Notions and Men's Apparel? Did old Mister Blitzstein have a boy that got killed in the war?"

"He sure did. Mort was with me. We were in

the same company — same platoon, as a matter of fact."

There was something in the way Lew Marsh said the words, that kept even twelve-year-old Rusty from asking any more questions — and trying to imagine, after all these years, the chill and noise of the Champagne Sector when Company C went up to the front.

Lew and Agnes took their places with other parents, far back on the crowded benches. There were even quite a few people standing. Lew told Agnes later that he really got a big kick out of the ceremony . . . there was the flag, and the arrowheads, and the sudden hush, and all that. . . . Of course, it was just kid stuff; but sometimes Lew thought there might be more to the Boy Scouts than appeared on the surface.

All those little kids in their sweaters and shirts, lined up before the Scoutmaster (he was Mr. McMurray who ran the big chicken hatchery, and he was proud and eager to be Scoutmaster) . . . holding up their hands with three fingers extended in the Scout salute . . . the other boys who were full-fledged Scouts, some of them tall brawny youths already playing football in high school, standing at attention in full uniform, watching the Tenderfeet being sworn in. . . .

"On my honor, I will do my best to do my duty to God and my country, and to obey the Scout law; to help other people at all times; and to keep myself physically strong, mentally awake, and morally straight."

Contests, afterward; and then the awarding of some honors, and two teams of the new boys demonstrating some of the tests which they had passed; and games; and finally refreshments which the Scouts had prepared themselves.

Everybody standing and singing:

> "My country, 'tis of thee,
> Sweet land of liberty,
> Of thee I sing — "

After the meeting, Lew walked through the courthouse park with Agnes and Rusty, leaving them to turn toward Willson Avenue and go home alone while he went down to the store to check up and close things for the night.

All that Rusty could talk about was a Scout axe. He was bound and determined to have one.

"Didn't you notice them, Pop? They're not a required thing — I mean, you don't *have* to have them — But they're swell . . . and a little leather case and everything, that fastens on your belt."

Lew said, doubtfully: "Well, I don't know. How much does a Scout axe cost?"

"The one I want costs two-eighty-five," said Rusty glibly.

Lew looked at him in the gloom. "Think you can save that much, very easily?"

Rusty swallowed. "I don't know. I'll try."

He did try, too. He had a hoard of pennies and nickels and dimes; he saved them in an empty baby-powder can hidden at the back of a shelf in the pharmacy chamber. The drugstore was just about as much home to Rusty as the house was.

Lew used to watch him, time and again, getting down that can to count over the money and see how close he was to attaining his axe. Rus went without a lot of things in order to get that little hoard together. Finally after a number of weeks, the total had reached two-forty-seven.

"Not very far to go now!" chortled Rusty, as he banged the can back up on the shelf.

It was early morning when he said this.

"Rusty," said his father, "will you be here awhile?"

"Sure. I don't have to leave for school for about another fifteen minutes."

Lew told him, "If Miss Emmy is busy waiting on trade out front, and I'm not yet back from the post office, you deliver that prescription there on the desk, if the customer comes in for it. It's all made up, and the amount's written on the package. I don't know the customer — Doctor McKee gave me the prescription — so be sure you get the cash."

Lew went to the post office and got his morning mail out of the box. On the way back up the alley he was reading letters, and one of them made him sore as a boil.

The Apex Supply Company had deliberately misinterpreted his order with regard to the refund, and so on. Well, he remembered he had kept a copy of that letter he wrote to them. . . .

He entered his store through the back door; and he was up on the little balcony above the rear room, looking through his office files, when he heard steps approaching that end of the store. He looked down.

Rusty came into the prescription room and took a professional stance inside the window, though he could barely see over the top.

"Yes, sir," he said to the customer. "I believe the prescription's here all right. What's the name, please?"

It was fun to stand there unobserved, and look down and see your son being such a man about things.

Lew could see through the window, even from that angle. He could see the customer: a flat-chested, round-shouldered man of sixty-five, with a haunted, stubbly face.

The customer said, "Watson, sonny. Sam Watson's my name. That there medicine is what the doctor said my wife was to have."

Rusty examined the little box. "That's right. 'S. Watson.' Two dollars and a quarter, Mr. Watson."

The man gulped, and put his hands on the broad sill. "I wonder, sonny," he asked, in a mild voice, "if maybe I could speak to the manager?"

Lew was about to sing out from his place on the balcony, but something kept him from it.

"Sorry, Mr. Watson," said Rusty. "My father isn't in right now. He told me to deliver the prescription when the customer called. And — and he said I was to get cash."

"Sonny." Old Watson's voice was a desperate whisper. "I ain't only got but — thirty-five cents. That's all I got to my name. I tell you, sonny, Mrs. Watson — She's having quite a little pain and — Well, now, I've heard of your father, and I guess he's an upstanding citizen. Well, do you suppose he'd mind trusting me for the other dollar-ninety? I'll maybe get some work next week, and —"

There was silence, during which Lew stood there and listened, and he heard two girls laughing up front by the magazine stand. Far away, the bell in the schoolhouse steeple was beginning to ring. Rusty would have to leave in a minute.

Rusty made a smothered sound. He reached out and drew in the thirty-five cents which Mr. Watson offered through the window.

"I guess," said Rusty, "that that'll be — all right with the manager."

The old man muttered something which sounded like, "God bless you, sonny," and went away weakly with the package grasped in his hand.

A board cracked under Lew's foot just then, but Rus never heard it. He was getting down the baby-powder can and slowly counting out one dollar and ninety cents, which he put with Mr. Watson's quarter and dime in the cash drawer.

Lew didn't say a word; just stood there and watched him do it, and saw him hurry away to school.

No, Lew didn't even mention it to Agnes. But that night, when Rusty went to crawl into bed, he turned back the sheet because he felt a big lump underneath. And there was a lump, all right. It was the Scout axe.

Rusty used that axe a long time. In memory now, Lew Marsh and Grampa could see the blade flashing through the years, and could hear its solid *chop, chop, chop.*

There was firewood to be cut, on overnight hikes where the Boy Scouts went . . . times when the boys sat in a cross-legged ring around the campfire and sang everything from "Sweet Genevieve" through "Down by the Old Mill Stream," up to and including that grim Depression ditty of modern times, "Brother, Can You Spare a Dime?" And the glorified campaign shout of 1936, when Rusty was an Eagle Scout, and the boys all sang, "Happy Days Are Here Again" . . .

The axe was used to split kindling for the old fireplace at home, too, on nights when there were parties. High school kids coming in . . . the battered golden-oak victrola squawking, or the old piano banging under its tasseled cover in the hall . . . again the kids were picking up Big Apple and jitterbug tunes out of some evening broadcast.

The axe was used to break ice for fruit punch, and to pound up windows when they stuck, and to tap against a wheel of the old car when Rusty was changing tires. Eventually the axe found its way down to the store; and there in the back room Rusty pried open the wooden packing-cases which came from wholesale houses . . . A strong axe — a good little axe. It seemed that the handle would never break.

"No, I suppose you wouldn't call him a religious boy," whispered Grampa to Lew Marsh, "but after all, what ordinary and normal American boy is extremely religious? When he was a Scout, he did his duty to God and his country just as he promised to do. It didn't mean that he had to grow up to be a missionary. Not necessarily."

Lew said: "One thing I do remember; he was treasurer of his Sunday-school class for a while."

"That's right," nodded Grampa. "I guess he made a good treasurer, if a reluctant one. And then, he always went to the young people's meetings a lot — Epworth League, and things like that."

"For a very good reason, too," said Lew.

They both giggled, and stood in shadows and watched a tall lean Rusty and a lot of other boys, hanging around on an early Sunday evening, watching to see which girls went into the church to young people's meeting; and then skulking in after them and joining, somewhat shame-faced and embarrassed, in all the talk about living worth-while lives and making their parents proud of them.

When the meeting broke up, that was the important thing. The boys got outside first, and lined up and waited for the girls. If you were already hooked up, through preference and habit, to some certain girl, you simply stepped up and took her arm and went away laughing with her.

But, on the other hand, if there were a new girl in town — say a remarkably pretty one, with long pale yellow hair, like Gretchen Porter — you had to nerve yourself to the ordeal. You stepped up and shuffled your feet, and were suddenly at a loss for words, and then said something about its being a nice night. And if Gretchen agreed that it was a nice night, and lingered to talk about it for a moment — why then, pretty soon you found yourself moving west through the chilly shadows of Bank Street with her. You may have been stepping in autumn leaves, but you thought you were really walking on the clouds.

It was a pretty good year, all in all — that last year of high school. Sometimes, generally speaking, it didn't seem as if there was a lot to do — for young people, that is — in a town like Hartfield. Of course there was always work at the store; and there were always lessons to prepare; and Rusty was taking a double dose of science at high school, so that meant a lot of extra work for him. He was trying to read some big pharmaceutical books, too, between times, down at the store.

He had an awful lot of interference with his reading.

Sure as he opened a book, there was bound to come a lot of giggling and wise-cracking and laughter: the front door of Marsh's would bang, and girls or boys would be ganged up around the soda fountain and around the record cabinets at the back of the store, and around Rusty always. . . . They called him "Doc" whenever they saw him with those big pharmaceutical books.

He wasn't heavy enough for football, though he tried out for the team, and they made a scrub out of him. He got to play two quarters in the game with Iowa Falls; then he hurt his shoulder and had to go around in a cast for about ten days, so that effectually stopped his football career.

Rusty did better in the spring when track season opened. The two-twenty hurdles: that was Rusty's dish. He got first in the sub-district, and later on managed to squeeze out a victory in the district meet, but was roundly beaten when Hart. field sent its track team to the state meet.

("I was proud of him," Lew whispered to Grampa. "I guess I was even prouder of him when he lost. He lost so damn well."

"Person's got to learn to lose well, just the same as win well," said Grampa, taking an emphatic bite out of his highly-seasoned tobacco plug.

"Wish I could have done more for him, though. . . ."

Grampa chewed serenely. "Don't see where you could have done any better. If an American small town isn't a good place for young folks to grow up in, then I'm suffering from delusions. We hear a lot of news, up there where I've been. But I never heard tell that MacArthur came from a big city. Admiral King was a small-town boy, and so was Wendell Willkie, and so was Eisenhower, and so was Harry Hopkins; and Henry Wallace came from Iowa. Lew, I guess you gave Rusty just about the best there was.")

Well, he gave him love and potato salad in Briggs' Woods, just as Lew himself had had them . . . and there was Rusty, holding fence wires so that a girl could crawl through and wander in the pasture with him.

Rus had some fishing in the Boone River, and the family Chev to drive sometimes on dates after he was big enough, and he had the free public library and the county fair, and street carnivals; and almost every year of his life he got to go to the big Lions' Club picnic — the Tri-County one, over at Fort Dodge — for Lew was a Lion, and the Tri-County picnic was one of the most important Roars of the year, and all the Lionesses and Cubs were invited along, too.

Lew and Agnes gave Rusty a thousand hours in which to dream and plan and plot his personal ambitions. They and their world offered him the bob-rides, on cold winter nights when snow was so deep that you would never have thought there was any pavement in town . . . when sleigh bells sang on the harness, and girls squealed and whispered in the straw of the bob-sled; and there was a chance to hold hands, to feel the warm and affectionate presence of another creature (a crea-

ture like yourself, but still bewitchingly different) underneath the blankets. The bob-rides
ended up invariably with oyster stew somewhere,
and hot chocolate, too; plenty of times those
oyster stews were served over the marble fountain at Marsh's.

The store was a modern store now. That was
the winter of early 1938, and Lew had installed
a lot of shiny chromium steam-table equipment.

Yes, Rusty had his work, and his private
thoughts, and his ordinary falls from grace, and
his decent acts of tenderness or superiority. He
had his girl, too. She was still the yellow-haired
Gretchen, though Lew privately didn't approve
of her very much because she was getting to be
such a flibberty-gibbet. She put on too much
make-up, and she dressed more expensively than
her family could really afford. Lew and Agnes
shook their heads about it, though naturally they
never let on to Rusty.

There came the end of the school year, and
the baccalaureate sermon at the church. It was a
fairly good sermon, such as should be delivered
to a high school class graduating into a world
where the name *Hitler* rang with shrill menace.

Privately, Agnes didn't feel that the sermon was as good as the one her own father might have delivered; but she was prejudiced.

They sat together, Lew and Agnes, and held hands like a couple of kids themselves, and watched the fifty-four members of the class file into the auditorium, singing.

But Rusty himself looked sober when he came down to the store about ten-thirty. Agnes had driven Lew downtown after the baccalaureate exercises were over, and had then gone on home. But naturally, Rusty had important business of his own. He had to take Gretchen home from the church.

He came into the store slowly, and Lew looked at him with pride through the prescription window, because Rusty had a new suit that he had earned himself — purchased it out of his own salary for part-time work at the store.

He wore the new shoes and necktie and hat which had been his father's graduation present.

"Going to close up soon, Pop?"

Lew glanced at the clock. "Any time now. You know I sort of make a habit of staying open until eleven on Fridays, just in case. . . . Those were pretty good exercises up at the church, Rusty."

"Yes," said Rusty, and that was all he would say; and pretty soon when Lew turned around he found that Rus had pulled on an old overall suit over his good clothes and was preparing to open a packing case.

Lew remonstrated. Said that it wasn't necessary.

"Oh," said Rusty, "I'd just as soon, while you're getting ready to close up. This box has got all those new bath salts in, and you know I wanted to make a big display early tomorrow, out there in the center for the Saturday trade."

For a while there wasn't much sound in the store except the crack and prying as Rusty worked with the little Boy Scout axe.

Lew cleared his throat. "Anything go wrong tonight, son?"

"Oh," said Rusty, "it was just Gretchen," and Lew's heart jumped.

"What happened?" He tried to make his question seem casual.

"It was just — about Sunday." After a while Rusty added: "I had a date with her for Sunday afternoon. We thought we'd go with some of the others down to Briggs' Woods, but — well, there's a guy works for her father . . . salesman or something, fellow about twenty-four, named Cliff Jeffers."

Lew said, "Yes, I know him. He's a customer here at the store," and his tone told much. After all, a druggist is something like a doctor; he knows a lot about the personal habits of people.

Rusty said: "This fellow Jeffers — he's got a real sweet car and he wanted to take Gretchen all the way down to Des Moines . . . I don't know, have supper and go to a movie or something. . . ."

Lew said, after a moment, "Rusty, Mother and I won't be needing the Chev. If you'd like to drive to Des Moines — "

"Hell, no," said Rusty decisively. "Didn't I tell you we were planning a picnic? Well, if that's the way she feels about it, she can damn well go to Des Moines! And she can damn well keep on going with Cliff Jeffers, for all I care."

Lew wanted to cheer. But just at that moment Rusty gave a vengeful pry to the last board of the box, and the handle of the little axe snapped and shivered.

Rusty looked at the slivery fragments. "Well, Pop, I guess that axe will have to have a new handle. Remember the day you gave it to me?"

"I sure do," said Lew.

A few minutes later they were walking home together through the warm night, and it seemed as if Rusty were another man and not just a boy. Lew offered him a cigarette and Rusty said, "No, thanks. Mind if I smoke my pipe?"

The pipe and the cigarette glowed like flowers along the darkness of Willson Avenue.

When they got home, while Rusty was sampling oatmeal cookies (Agnes always left something out on the table when they came in late), Lew went down cellar and pretty soon he came back with a bottle of homemade loganberry wine. An old lady made it, there in Hartfield, and sometimes she gave Lew a few bottles when she wasn't able to pay her little bill at the store.

Lew filled two sherbet cups — Agnes got those from her aunt for a wedding present, he remembered. He filled them solemnly with the sweet dark wine, and he and Rusty drank in silence and in pride.

After Lew got into bed beside Agnes it took him a long while to go to sleep. He didn't hear a sound from Rusty's room, but he had a hunch that Rus wasn't asleep either. Maybe in this sudden maturity, Rusty was just as proud of being a man as Lew was to have him be one.

Now that he had become a man he didn't necessarily put away all the childish things he once had loved.

"Funny thing," said Grampa, nodding through mists of recollection to Lew, as together they watched Rusty packing ice-cream into a dry-pack container to carry along on his inevitable Sunday picnic. "Funny thing — but the man who makes a clean sweep and puts all childish things away forever — somehow he becomes less a man than the one who always remains a little childish in some ways."

Certainly Rusty still enjoyed picnics, though he didn't take Gretchen to any more of them. He sort of shopped around among girls there in town; and he was always the eligible boy who gets asked for a blind date when there comes a visiting niece from Omaha, or a new young teacher in the kindergarten.

It took him about a year to settle his affections in any particular direction, and then he settled them right next door.

The Prentiss family lived there, long-time neighbors of Agnes and Lew; and they had a daughter whom Rusty never noticed except with loathing, when he was in high school. . . . If he wanted to make an invidious comparison he'd say: "Gosh! She looks just about as bad as Lenore Prentiss," or, "Lenore Prentiss and a lot of awful girls like that. . . ."

But by the fall of 1938, Lenore Prentiss herself was an upperclassman in high school. And the next thing anyone knew, Charley Prentiss made a good chunk of money and got a fine promotion in his insurance organization, and to the amazement of the neighborhood he sent Lenore off to a fancy junior college, a regular girls' school in Missouri. It was something like an Eastern finishing school, people said.

When Lenore came back she was quite a different person; at least Rusty thought so. She wasn't beautiful: just the regular type of American girl with a good-looking body and a full, laughing mouth and level gray-green eyes. She wasn't pretty, but she was young, and her hair shone.

Rusty took her out a good deal that summer. Of course, he went with other girls when Lenore wasn't in Hartfield; they weren't engaged or anything like that; they were just young people having a good time. Rusty saved up and bought a croquet set — a heavy, modern set — with a rubber face on one end of every mallet-head. Rusty worked early Sunday mornings, leveling the ground in the back yard until it was as smooth as a pool table; he and his mother planted a special grass there and tended the new sod carefully. The resulting croquet ground was the delight of youthful Hartfield.

Mallets clacked all summer long, and heavy balls whistled through the thick steel wickets — or bounced disappointingly off the edges. A portable radio chanted under the grape arbor. Agnes made chicken and bologna sandwiches in the kitchen, until Rusty rebelled and carried Agnes outside, squealing and struggling like a young girl herself; and he threw her into the hammock and tied the edges to imprison her. He said that hereafter he and the gang would make their own sandwiches. . . .

Croquet balls pounded across the turf, evenings and holidays, and catbirds meowed under the gooseberry bushes. Then suddenly the radio songs were stilled. Men's taut voices filled the ether.

Hitler had gone crushing into Poland.

A few nights later, at the store, Rusty spoke with Lew in the back room. He said that a lot of the boys were talking about going up to Canada and getting into this thing. Arch Birmingham, for instance: he was quite an intellectual, for all that he was a good amateur welterweight, too. Sometimes when he and Rusty were younger, and momentarily mad at their little world, they had talked about running away to Spain and joining the fight there. But Arch wasn't a kid any longer. And he was bound and determined to get into this war.

Bud Flanagan and Peter Orcutt both had their private pilot's licenses . . . they said that they thought they would go up to Winnipeg or somewhere and join the Canadian flying corps.

"I suppose that means you've got a notion you want to go with them, Rusty?" asked Lew.

Rus shook his head. "Not exactly. But you know, a lot of us were talking last night, and we've got a hunch that this thing is going to go a lot further and last a lot longer than most people around here think. No, I'm no pilot, and maybe I wouldn't even be very good with a gun."

He laughed. "You know, I never shot anything but a .22. Rats and tin cans and things. . . ."

Lew carefully dampened a poison label and put it on a little bottle which he had just filled with white capsules. "Yes," he said easily, "wars are an unsettling business."

Rusty muttered, "It makes a guy feel like he wants to do something . . . kind of get straightened around and head for somewhere."

Lew told him: "We talked about college last year. I offered to help you down at Ames or Iowa U. or anywhere else. But you said you didn't want to."

Rusty snapped a rubber band at his father, and Lew ducked.

Rus said, "We talked about medicine, but I don't feel any ambition to be a doctor. I'd waste your investment and my own energy. Perhaps I'd be frittering away half my time, all because I didn't have any business in medical school. It makes me sick the way some guys go down there and spend a lot of dough and then come back, after a year or two, just where they left off. I guess I was some help to you in the store, wasn't I?"

Lew shrugged. "Well, maybe, just a little! Say, I'd have had to pay two extra people at least a hundred dollars a month apiece to do what you've done around here this year. I didn't pay you anything like that."

"O. K.," said Rusty. "Now look, Pop, I'm pretty well up in my pharmacopoeia. If you can get along without me for a while, I'll go down to the Des Moines School of Pharmacy and get busy. Eventually I'll qualify for my license. If the war's over and the world is running smoothly, I'll be set to do some real good for the store and myself too. We might even buy old Granville's grocery building next door, and make one side of this place into a high-class luncheonette and confectionery place, and the other side all drugs and sundries, the way you've talked about doing sometimes."

Lew wrapped the bottle, and put a rubber band around it. "If the world isn't at peace and running smoothly, what about that?"

Rusty was silent for a moment. Then he said: "I guess I'll be a lot more good to the army or navy or marines or somebody — I guess I'll be worth more to them as a skilled technician, even in pharmacy, than I will as an unskilled recruit. What do you say, Pop?"

Lew felt warm and valiant. He felt something like he did the first day he saw Agnes . . . or farther back, the day he was made a corporal in the infantry long ago.

"I say," he cried, "that you'd better plan to go down to Des Moines to the College of Pharmacy."

When he and Rusty got home that night they drank some loganberry wine.

In 1941 the world wasn't at peace, and it wasn't running smoothly.

When Rusty was at home, working in the store

that summer, Lew mentioned having made some conversation with old man Granville about the grocery building next door; not an actual proposition, not in so many words — but he edged around the subject a little.

That was just bait. He wanted to see how Rus would react to it.

Rusty reacted, all right. He came out in the yard on Sunday evening in the twilight, as Lew was finishing watering the flowers with the hose.

"Pop, maybe you'd better not talk any more to Mr. Granville."

"Why not? Don't you think that would be a good proposition?"

"In ordinary times, yes. But these aren't ordinary times."

"I guess not," muttered Lew. "Not when you look at the papers, or listen to the radio and hear what's happening in Russia and places like that."

"Don't forget the Pacific," said Rusty.

Lew squirted a fine spray from the hose toward old Biff — not getting him wet, just teasing him — and Biff dodged and made a challenging sound.

Lew asked, "Why do you mention the Pacific?"

"Little brown men no like Amelicans," said Rusty, making a queer face and pretending that he was a Japanese, although he had never actually seen a Japanese.

Then he burst out: "What's the use of waiting to be drafted? Maybe if everybody keeps on waiting we'll find we've waited too long!"

His father went up to the house and turned off the hydrant. He unscrewed the hose, and Rusty began to reel it up on its little wooden cart.

"O.K.," Lew told him. "What's it going to be, big boy; army, navy or marines?"

"You sound kind of resentful about the marines," said Rusty, looking at him. "How come?"

"Never mind," said Lew, and he couldn't help grinning to himself. "What's it going to be? Maybe the air corps?"

"Sure," laughed Rusty. "Pharmacy ought to help me a lot, there! No, Pop, I'll tell you. It's kind of silly, but — Well, I always did want to see the ocean."

It was getting dark. Lew watched Rusty wheeling the hose reel into the tool-shed next to the garage. After Rusty came to meet him by the grape arbor, and as they walked to the house together, Lew said, "Go ahead! Join the navy, and see a lot of oceans!"

"Wonder if I'll get seasick?" meditated Rusty.

"I know I did, in the last war!" said Lew. Already unconsciously people were calling it that. "Twice. I got sick as a dog going over, and coming back."

They walked into the house. Lew went to hunt for the loganberry wine, but it was all gone.

"Looked real good in his uniform," whispered Grampa.

"Yes. . . ."

"Sailors' uniforms," said Grampa, "haven't changed as much since the Civil War as the army has. 'Course, I never saw many sailors, not where I was — with the Third Iowa. But after the war, sometimes, at G. A. R. encampments — "

Lew put his hand on Grampa's sleeve. "Look," he said, "look at Lenore Prentiss, will you? She's saying that his uniform is cute; isn't that just like a girl? They go for a sailor every time, if you give them half a chance."

"Do you reckon he and Lenore were engaged, Lew?"

Lew shook his head.

"Or maybe in love," pursued Grampa, "or — "

Lew said, "Maybe Agnes would know more about that than I would. I'd hazard a guess that they liked each other a lot but — I don't know. If he had come back, why maybe — You can't tell about such things."

Grampa rolled his tobacco in his mouth. "It's a kind of wisdom, Lew," he said, "when a man admits ignorance in such a case."

The bus pulled out, the bus bound for Des Moines, and Rusty waved a freckled hand at the window. And then he was gone, and that was the end of Rusty (wailed Lew to himself, clenching his fists) and that was the end of everything.

Grampa walked so silently beside Lew now, strolling back toward the old house, that Lew wondered if Grampa might not be reading his thoughts.

". . . As long as kids can play Indian in the corn," whispered Grampa.

Lew stopped and looked at him. "What did you say?"

Grampa kept walking. He stopped to poke among the clovers at a certain place along the parking, with the tip of his cane. Lew remembered that: a little weakness of the old man. He used to stop there, almost square in front of the Andrews house, every day when he went past. He would spend a minute or two looking for four-leaf clovers. Sometimes he found one, and put it in his little pocket notebook. There were many such four-leaf clovers, drying and brown, staining the pages of the old drug register down at the store.

Lew kept plaguing Grampa. . . . "What's that about playing Indian in the corn?"

"Did I talk about corn?" asked Grampa mildly. "Must have been thinking out loud. . . . Remember this, Lew: as long as American boys can be Boy Scouts, as long as they can eat ice-cream, as long as they can do a good turn daily, as long as they can go to high school, or play football, or have a picnic in Briggs' Woods . . . as long as they can feel impelled to take a hard-saved dollar-and-ninety-cents out of a baby-powder box — "

Lew was puzzled. "As long as all those things, then — what?"

"It'll be worth while," said Grampa.

"What'll be worth while?"

"A guy named Rusty," said Grampa. "A lot of kids like that, with a lot of names."

Lew Marsh felt all choked up inside. He wanted to shout and say, "What are you trying to do? Tell me I ought to be glad because my own son was killed in the war?" . . . Sometimes he and Grampa used to have arguments, pretty spicy ones; though Grampa hadn't licked him after he was ten or eleven. Maybe he hadn't needed to be licked, but —

Well, there was no sense in offending the old man — especially since he said he had gone to so much trouble to get permission from the Authorities, and all that. And since he had been so nice about taking Lew for a stroll around town.

It was a stroll that had lasted twenty-odd years, though by modern Hartfield time it consumed only a few hours.

Here they were now, back where they started, lingering in front of the kind old house, halting for a moment to listen to a mourning-dove up in that big maple somewhere.

Lew cleared his throat. "Gramp, it's getting on toward suppertime. It's kind of an awkward situation. I don't know quite how to handle it, with Agnes not able to notice you and — But if you wanted to stay, and sit down to supper with us, why — "

Grampa laughed. "You forget, Lew," he said, "you forget my peculiar condition."

Lew felt embarrassed. To cover his confusion he said, "Well, anyway, let's go round in back. I imagine Agnes is out there watering her flowers. It takes quite a while, now that we haven't got any hose; but she says she thinks that old-time watering-can is pretty picturesque, anyway."

They went round the corner of the house, out past the syringa bushes and the bird bath and Biff's kennel; and sure enough, there was Agnes, wearing a pair of old tennis shoes and a pink apron and managing to look pretty picturesque herself.

"Why, Lew Marsh," scolded Agnes (but in

some delight, as if she were pleased that he had gotten out and taken a good long walk). "Where on earth have you been? Aren't you all tired out?"

Lew smiled at her slowly. "Not at all. Fact is, I feel better than I've felt in some weeks."

He cleared his throat again. "Fact is, after supper I thought I might go down to the store and get busy."

He turned to see how Grampa would take this, because Agnes was obviously so tickled at his change of heart. But Grampa wasn't there.

Old Biff came and rubbed against Lew's legs . . . Grampa wasn't anywhere around.

Lew looked all over, and then he saw him. Grampa was going up the long slope past the Mansfield house. He stopped, with bright orange sunset light around him, and when he saw Lew looking, he waved his cane. Then he turned and kept on going, away up to the head of Prospect Street, up to a wide park-like hill. That was where he was going — under old elms and black pines, up there where little flags flapped and whistled on their staffs above the soldiers' graves.

It was after ten o'clock that night when Lew had to admit frankly that he was tired. Except for bookkeeping work, he hadn't really done anything much in weeks — and only a few hours of books.

But something struck him tonight, the moment he entered the store. He saw immediately a dozen things he wanted to change. He saw a hundred frayed edges that had developed during his reclusion . . . a kind of fringe on the abstract structure of the store, which needed his skill for the clipping.

Scarcely could he feel the friendly pressure of hands that reached for his across the counter. . . . Old Judge Colvin: they had quarreled, he and Lew, over the extension of the gas main out on Willson Avenue, and Judge Colvin hadn't shaken hands with him in years, though he always brought his business to that store because it was the best. . . . Now the judge let his bright black eyes soften under their tufted brows, and he reached his fat soft hand across the counter past a big pile of Kleenex, and he said: "Well, Lew, how're you doing?" and then nodded again before he went away with his purchases. Lew felt a warmth toward Judge Colvin. Suddenly, as his spirit embraced this petulant old enemy, he found that it was embracing all of Hartfield with new eagerness.

Still, he scarcely felt the physical touch of these people upon him. He was inspired, rather than depressed, by the trivia of his own existence. He wanted to get that cracked glass fixed, at the end of the perfume counter; and the electric ventilating fan in the rear wall was clicking again and needed oiling. Those patent medicines looked ugly, there so close to the toilet soaps and face powder, and why hadn't he ever thought to change them over to the shadowy shelves on the opposite side? Chris could do it just as well the next morning, but it seemed to Lew Marsh that the task should be performed now.

So he was working there . . . the night watchman came in and bought cigarettes, and Doc McKee stopped by to pick up some codeine. It was after ten o'clock. Lew sold two sodas and a hot fudge sundae and a chocolate malt to some kids homeward bound from the movies; then he rubbed off the top of the fountain and washed the few dishes and glasses.

He heard the ten-thirteen train come in, over
on the I.C., and he remembered the two or three
times that he and Rusty had escorted Agnes to
that very train, when she went to visit her folks
in Rockford, Illinois.

Lew pressed a switch: the whole front of
Marsh's went dark. That was the go-to-bed signal
. . . when people saw those lights out, over the
fountain and cigar and magazine counters, they
knew that Marsh's was officially closed for the
evening. The door was always left unlocked until
Lew actually went home, just in case, so he
wouldn't have to go and unfasten it to let in a
doctor or somebody. He was perfectly willing to
wait on stray customers, too — even gum-buying
customers, right up to the last minute — just so
they didn't want any sodas.

Now he would finish putting those ugly patent
medicine packages — the ugly labels, the phoney
panaceas which he hated to sell, though people
eternally demanded them — he would finish in-
stalling them in their new home on the high dark
shelves, and then he would go home himself.

Mounted on a step-ladder and holding a basket
on his arm for convenience as he worked, Lew

carefully placed the orange-and-black boxes of Father Tom's Magic Emulsion in front of each other.

He heard the front door open, but he couldn't turn around and crane his neck past the pipe display without endangering his perch on the ladder. . . . Lew Marsh thought he knew the step of half the people who came in the store, and he wondered whose step this was. Sounded like Tommy Glenn or Dave Boylston; he wasn't sure which.

He was just about to sing out, "Hey, Tommy," or, "Hey, Dave," when someone halted behind him.

An unfamiliar voice, and rather strained, asked: "Is this Marsh's?"

Lew turned around on the ladder and he got a brief shock. The young fellow who addressed him wore the uniform of the United States Navy, and that in itself was a real wallop for Lew just then.

He put his hand on the shelf. He knocked off one bottle of Father Tom's, but it only fell as far as the counter ledge and didn't break.

The young fellow took off his cap; there was a

manner of salute in the way he did it. He was a steady-faced youth with a strong thick neck and round gray eyes that fairly looked a hole through Lew Marsh. His face was extremely sunburnt, and you could see where he had had a recent haircut, because the close-cropped area around his temples wasn't tanned at all.

"Evening," said Lew. "Yes, this is Marsh's."

The sailor looked at him a while. Then he said, "I guess you're Rusty's father, aren't you?"

Lew got down off the ladder blindly. He stood there with the package of patent medicine in his hands. "What do you know about Rusty?"

The boy had two little bars of ribbon on his left breast; Lew didn't know it then, but he found out later: one of those was the ribbon of the Navy Cross.

"I'm Anton Cavrek," and the name meant nothing to the buzzing ears of Lew Marsh.

He looked down through the top and side glass of the counter, and he could see the shiny black shoes that the stranger wore below his blue uniform pants.

There was a little zipper bag on the floor beside him.

"Any friend of — Are you — ?"

The round gray eyes blinked two or three times. "I'm Tony. I thought maybe Rusty had said something about me in his letters and — "

. . . All the way back to the time when Rusty was at the recruit depot.

Got acquainted with a pretty nice guy this week, from Chicago. His name is Tony. When we got liberty, night before last, we. . . .

I wish you could enjoy the view from that big hotel in San Francisco like I did. It's certainly beautiful. Tony and I were up there Sunday afternoon, and had some beer in the bar on the roof, and just looked out of the windows. . . .

At the U. S. O. dance last week, Tony and I met a couple of real nice girls. We had liberty ashore on Sunday again, and went out to one of the girls' houses. She had a remarkable collection of records, and we surely —

Lew said flatly, "So you're Tony."

"Yes, sir."

"For goodness sake."

They shook hands among the Kleenex, but this was different from shaking hands with Judge

Colvin. . . . Lew didn't want to let go of Tony Cavrek's hand.

"Let's see," he said, "seems to me Rusty said your home was in Chicago?"

The boy nodded. "Yes, sir." His voice was smooth and low, but still strong and alert. "Such a home as I've got, I mean to say, sir. See, I've been an orphan since I was sixteen; but of course I kept on living in Chicago until I joined the navy."

He glanced around the store and Lew thought that he saw approval in Tony's gaze, or at least some kind of satisfaction. "I don't know whether Rusty told you," said Tony Cavrek, "but you know I used to jerk sodas in Chicago. This does seem familiar. You got a nice fountain there, Mr. Marsh."

It didn't seem right somehow to stay behind the counter any longer. But there were the bottles of patent medicine —

Tony understood at once, when Lew glanced up at the shelves. Then he was around the counter before you could wink, and up on the step-ladder.

"Here, just hand them up to me," and in a few moments the job was done.

Lew Marsh thanked him. "Want a cigar?"

"I wouldn't mind."

Lew started toward the cigar counter. But the sailor said: "Where do you keep this ladder?" and Lew pointed out the back room.

He went on up to the cigar counter and got out the best cigars he could find. They were three-for-fifty-cent coronas; Judge Colvin and Dave Boylston and a very few other men in Hartfield smoked cigars like that.

Lew got out two cigars, and when Tony joined him they lit up.

"Gee," said Tony, "this is a swell cigar! I don't very often smoke cigars, sir. You know how it is: cigarettes usually. But this is sure swell."

"Look here," said Lew, "are you bound for Chicago? When do you have to leave?"

Tony said that he didn't have to leave at any special time. . . . He had a trick of dropping his eyes for a moment and then they'd come up clear and strong, and you'd feel them going through you again.

"You see, Mr. Marsh, it was like this: Rusty

and I used to talk about — about what might happen and — See, I haven't got any folks or anything; but Rusty always said that if anything happened — I mean, to him — he said I ought to come when I got a chance and — call on you and his mother — "

There was a misty silence. It wasn't the silence of an empty store, but a place populated with many people, all of whom seemed to be holding their breath and waiting for something.

"You came in on the ten-thirteen from the west?"

"Yes, sir. I came from a Pacific port; sorry I can't tell you the name. But I still got the better part of two weeks ahead of me before I have to go back."

Lew said, "Well." Then he thought of the telephone. "I guess maybe I'd better call up — Rusty's mother — before we leave the store here. And tell her we're coming. . . ."

"Yes, sir," said Tony.

Lew made the call, and then the store was locked. In a few minutes he and Tony were moving south along the dark woodsy tunnel of Willson Avenue.

Lew pointed out the Congregational and Baptist churches, and he told Tony that the Methodist church, where they belonged, was a block over west.

"I was raised a Catholic, kind of," said Tony Cavrek.

"Oh, yes," said Lew, quickly. "You know, Father Frein here in Hartfield is one of my best friends and customers."

When they approached the house Agnes had lights turned on in the living room and in the kitchen, too; probably she was fixing something to eat.

Lew halted, just before they turned up the walk, and pointed out the big maple tree on the parking. "Rusty used to tap that," and Tony wanted to know what *tap* was.

"You bore a hole," said Lew. "Then the sap comes out. The kids used to call it sugar-water, and they liked to drink it."

"I bet it's good," said Tony Cavrek. "You know how it is in Chicago, on the west side. We didn't have any such sugar-water things."

Lew asked him: "You like to play croquet? I mean the modern kind, with great big mallets and heavy balls? We've got a swell set here . . . hasn't been used much lately."

They reached the steps. "I guess it would be swell," Tony said. "I would have to have somebody show me, though. I used to box some at the *Sokol* — that's a kind of club — and I play handball. That's about the only games I know much about."

"Well," said Lew, opening the screen door, "I guess Lenore Prentiss — she's a girl lives next door — I guess maybe she could show you."

They went into the house. Agnes began to cry; then she kissed Tony Cavrek. Lew went into the front room by the bay window and cried a little himself, just for a moment.

He came back, blowing his nose heartily and saying: "Well, well, well! Mother, where we going to put this big tramp of a sailor?"

Agnes wiped her eyes and smiled. "I guess you know where." She looked at Lew. "If he wants to . . ."

Tony's strong gray eyes were blinking rapidly. "It is O.K. by me, Mrs. Marsh," he said, and his mild voice seemed to ring through the rooms.

"I was just getting some lunch," said Agnes.

They followed her out in the kitchen and stood watching as she sliced the cold meat-loaf.

Lew said, "I wonder . . . maybe we'd better discuss it now. Is there anything you ought to tell us, Tony?"

The sailor stood very straight before them, and they watched his chest moving in its strong, easy breath behind the bright slabs of medal ribbon. He said, "You understand that I can't tell you where it was. I guess you know the date, maybe. When you got your telegram . . . ?"

Lew nodded. Somehow he didn't feel like crying any more.

"They came over awfully fast," said Tony. "We weren't surprised, but they had more planes than us; and a lot of them got through and began pounding us — our boat, I mean — pretty hard. Rusty and I were both topside to begin with, but he was ordered down to the sick bay right away. I saw him once, about twenty minutes later, when I had to go down there for a minute. . . . He was working hard, helping the doctors. They had a lot of wounded coming in, and I think Rusty saved quite a few lives. He was real good at his job."

Tony Cavrek looked at the kitchen stove, and seemed to be counting the little handles of the gas switches. Then he repeated slowly, "Rusty was real good — at any job he had to do."

He went on and told them: "An aerial torpedo came in on that side. It exploded through a couple of decks. They said Rusty was helping carry out some of the guys that were hurt, when he got it. I guess there isn't very much more I can tell you, except that I thought quite a lot of Rusty."

He stopped abruptly. . . . Finally Lew went over, and made a fist out of his hand, and hit Tony lightly two or three times on the shoulder. "You like loganberry wine?" he asked. "There's an old lady here in town makes it, and she gave me a couple of bottles last week."

"I guess I never had any loganberry wine," said Tony Cavrek, "but I bet it sure would be swell."

On Sale Now!

On Sale Now!

For more information
visit: www.speakingvolumes.us

On Sale Now!

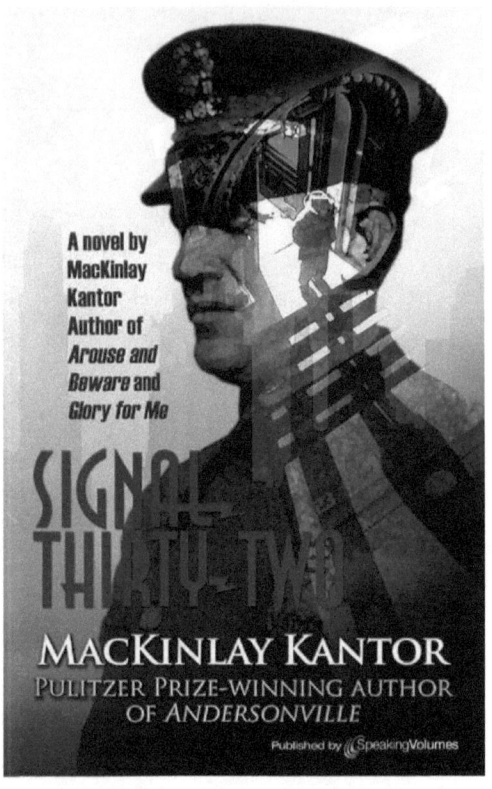

**For more information
visit:** www.speakingvolumes.us

On Sale Now!

BASIS FOR THE FILM
THE MAN FROM DAKOTA

For more information
visit: www.speakingvolumes.us

On Sale Now!

A NOVEL ABOUT A KILLER—BY THE AUTHOR OF
MIDNIGHT LACE & FRONTIER
Basis for the movie Hannah Lee: *An American Primitive*

WICKED WATER

MacKINLAY KANTOR
PULITZER PRIZE-WINNING AUTHOR
OF *ANDERSONVILLE*

Published by SpeakingVolumes

For more information
visit: www.speakingvolumes.us